Michael Arvaarluk Kusugak

ARCTIC STORIES

Vladyana Langer Krykorka

Annick Press Ltd.

Toronto • New York

THE CANADA COUNCIL | LE CONSEIL DES ARTS
FOR THE ARTS | DU CANADA
SINCE 1957 | DEPUIS 1957

We acknowledge the support of the Canada Council
for the Arts for our publishing program.
We also thank the Ontario Arts Council.

The author would like to thank Kathleen Keil for retyping these stories
when his computer dumped them from its memory.

The artist would like to thank Rhoda Karetak,
of Rankin Inlet, for her decorative borders.

Cataloguing in Publication Data

Kusugak, Michael
Arctic stories

ISBN 1-55037-453-2 (bound)   ISBN 1-55037-452-4 (pbk.)

1. Inuit — Northwest Territories—Repulse Bay—Juvenile fiction. 2. Children's stories,
Canadian (English).* I. Krykorka, Vladyana. II. Title.

PS8571.U83A83 1998   jC813'.54   C98-930202-4
PZ7.K87Ar 1998

The art in this book was rendered in watercolours and coloured pencil.
The text was typeset in Trumpet Lite.

Distributed in Canada by:
Firefly Books Ltd.
3680 Victoria Park Avenue
Willowdale, ON
M2H 3K1

Published in the U.S.A. by Annick Press (U.S.) Ltd.
Distributed in the U.S.A. by:
Firefly Books (U.S.) Inc.
P.O. Box 1338
Ellicott Station
Buffalo, NY 14205

Printed in Hong Kong.

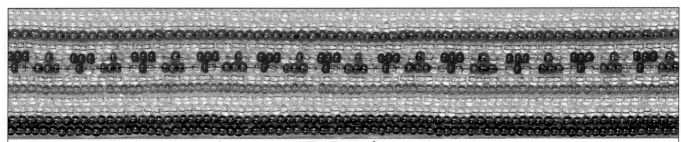

To Betanie

–M.A.K.

To Ortwin, for being there

–V.L.K.

✳

Prologue

In the summer of 1958[1] a helium-filled airship called a ZPG-2 took off from the US Navy Air Development Centre in South Weymouth, Massachusetts. It flew to Akron, Ohio and to Ottawa, Ontario and finally landed in Churchill, Manitoba. At 8:30 in the morning, on the 7th of August, it again floated into the air like a giant, oblong balloon. It floated aloft, 300 metres in the air, heading north. It flew to a giant, floating piece of ice with a very scientific name: T-3.

On T-3 were scientists from Canada, the United States, Russia and other countries all over the world. They were studying ice, things that cling to ice floes, and the way ice moves with the currents in Alaska and northern Canada. The scientists were very busy people.

The job of the people in the airship was to draw very accurate maps of northern Canada. The airship was 106 metres long and 33 metres high. It looked a lot like a big, black bomb with fins on the back. In the gondola attached to its belly was a Royal Canadian Air Force Wing Commander, Keith Greenaway. He was the navigator. In his journal he wrote: "We noticed several polar bears on the pans of ice off Chesterfield Inlet. As soon as the airship approached, they became panic stricken, diving and swimming in one direction then the other."

Not long after it left Churchill, the giant, black airship flew over a tiny community on the Arctic Circle called Repulse Bay. And, like the polar bears on the ice floes, we were really scared.

[1]Wing Commander K.R. Greenaway, "To the Top of the World by Airship," The Roundell (May 1960), p.14.

Agatha and the Ugly Black Thing

It was spring in Repulse Bay. As Agatha slept in her bright igloo, a drop of water hung on the ceiling, just above her head. The snow was melting. The water dropped on her big, fat cheek. Agatha rolled over and opened one eye. She looked up at the ceiling. She saw another drop, ready to fall. She closed her eye and waited. She heard a small creak, like the sound of walking on hard snow. Oh, oh! she thought. And then the roof came crashing down.

The whole igloo had fallen down. There was snow on the bed, snow on her sleeping bag and snow on her face. There was snow everywhere. She was not inside her igloo anymore; she was outside, in the bright sunshine.

"Time to get up," her mother said.

Agatha put her head inside her sleeping bag. "I am staying right here," she said. Agatha loved to sleep. Her friends thought she was lazy, but she wasn't, really. She just loved to sleep. Sleeping was her hobby.

"We are going to put up our tent," her mother said. "Come and help."

"But I want to sleep," she said.

"All right, but you will be here, outside, all by yourself," her mother said.

"Okay, I'm coming," Agatha said, and got up.

Agatha's father carried the tent to a bare patch of gravelly ground on the beach. "We will pitch it here," he said. And that is where they spent the summer.

It was a glorious summer. Repulse Bay is a tiny bay at the northern tip of Hudson Bay. In summer, the sea is a nice blue-green colour until the uugait come. Uugait are tiny black fish with little beards on their chins. So many of them come into Repulse Bay in summer that the whole bay turns black. Whales like to follow the uugait.

Hundreds of whales would swim in the tiny bay, diving, surfacing and blowing air out through the tops of their heads, chasing the tiny black fish. There were white beluga whales. There were spotted grey narwhals with their long spirally tusks. And, sometimes, even killer whales would come into the bay.

The whales made strange noises: "Drrr, drr..." They splashed water: Splash, splash! They breathed air out through the tops of their heads: Poooohhff. They made a lot of noise. Agatha would fall asleep watching them. She dreamed about floating in the water with the whales.

Sometimes, early in the morning when the sun was very bright, Agatha's father played the record player. The record player was a little wooden box. Her father opened it up, attached a shiny needle to it, turned the crank on the side and played his records. Agatha dreamed she was watching all the people praying in Father Didier's church. She dreamed she was watching from heaven and all the angels were singing:

> Oh, ye'll take the high road
> And I'll take the low road
> And I'll be in Scotland before ye
> But me and my true love will never meet again
> On the bonnie, bonnie banks of Loch Lomond...

She would wake up and there would be her father, playing the record player.

And Agatha would smile at her father, close her eyes and go back to sleep. Ah, it was so peaceful. Only the whales and the birds and Agatha's father's record player made noises. They were nice noises. But that summer, August 7, 1958 was not such a good day to have sleeping as a hobby. People were running on the gravel outside. She heard them yelling, "It's coming. It's coming!"

"Be quiet!" Agatha yelled back at them.

But people kept running and yelling, "It's coming, it's coming!"

Agatha got up. She went outside. It was a beautiful day. She looked around. People were everywhere, looking south, yelling, "It's coming, it's coming."

Agatha looked south. There was nothing there. She went over to her father. "What's coming, Father?" she asked.

Her father pointed south and said, "That."

Agatha looked. She did not see anything at all.

Her father pointed at the horizon.

Agatha looked and looked. She scrunched up her eyes and looked some more. Sure enough, just above the horizon Agatha saw a tiny black speck.

"What is it?" she asked.

Her father said, "I don't know. But it's coming."

Agatha looked and looked at the tiny black speck and, sure enough, it was coming.

The thing grew and grew. It was black. It was an oblong kind of thing. It looked like a giant avataq, a sealskin float, with fins on the back. It had a little building kind of thing stuck to the bottom of it. It was huge. And it was coming.

The people ran here, they ran there, not knowing which way to run. They screamed and yelled, "What is it?"

The answer was the same: "I don't know, but it's coming!"

Agatha looked at the thing with her big brown eyes. "It's ugly," she said.

An old man sat on a rock, looking at the thing, thinking. He pointed a crooked old finger at it. "I have heard..." he said in an old, gravelly voice. He was in no hurry. "I have heard, way over on the other side of the ocean...there is a big war. I have heard..." He paused and coughed a bit.

And the thing kept coming. It loomed over Repulse Bay. It made a noise like an airplane. It looked like it was coming down on the tiny community, right down on the people.

The old man spoke again. "I have heard they drop big, black round qaaqtaqtut, exploding-things, that explode when they hit the ground. Maybe, just maybe, this thing is one of those exploding-things and it is coming to get us. Just maybe."

And the people got really scared and started running away. They could not run west; there were hills there. They could not run east; there is a cliff there. And the sea lies to the east of the cliff. So they ran north, away from the thing.

"Come!" Agatha's father said.

"Come!" her mother said.

Agatha ran over the rocks. She ran over the hummocks, she ran over the tiny flowers that covered the ground and she ran over puddles. She ran as fast as she could. Everybody was running, all the people from Repulse Bay. And still the big black thing kept coming. It was right above them.

Agatha was tired. She did not want to run anymore. She wanted to stop and take a nap. She was tired and hot. And she was mad at the thing for waking her from her dreams.

She stopped. She turned around and crossed her arms on her chest. She looked up at the thing and said, "Hummph!"

Her father said, "Come!"

Her mother said, "Come!"

Agatha said, "I'm tired."

The thing kept coming. Agatha was mad, really mad. She yelled at the thing, "Go away!"

The thing seemed to stop right over her head.

Agatha waved her fist at it. She was so mad. She started running back, waving her fist, yelling, "Go away, go away, you…YOU… UGLY…BLACK…THING!"

The thing seemed to stop, trying to decide what to do.

"Go away, YOU UGLY BLACK THING!" Agatha kept yelling.

And sure enough, the thing slowly started to go away, heading north. Agatha ran after it, yelling, "Go away, you, you UGLY BLACK THING!"

The thing kept going. It got smaller and smaller. Finally it became a tiny black speck at the other end of the horizon from where it had come. And then it disappeared.

Agatha yelled after it, "And don't come back!"

And the ugly black thing never flew over Repulse Bay again.

All the people were tired too. They sat on the rocks to rest. Agatha's father picked her up and carried her back to the people.

All the people yelled, "Hurray! Hurray for Agatha! Hurray for Agatha for saving the day!"

But Agatha did not hear them. She had her head on her father's shoulder and her thumb in her mouth. She was fast asleep.

Taimakalauq

14

Agatha
and the Most Amazing Bird

Agatha walked with her grandmother on hard snow. "Crunch, crunch, crunch..." went her feet.

"Crunch, crunch, crunch..." went her grandmother's feet.

The wind blew on her face. It was cold, very cold. Her cheeks were cold; her nose was cold. She turned around, pulled her hand out of her mitten and put it on her cheek to warm it.

She walked along beside her grandmother, backwards. Hopping along, following them, was a big black bird. Agatha asked, "Grandmother, what is that bird?"

"It is a tulugarjuaq," her grandmother replied. "A raven."

"It's ugly," Agatha said.

It was ugly, the ugliest bird Agatha had ever seen. Except for the frost on its beak, it was black from the top of its head to the tips of its tail feathers. It had wide black wings with black fingers on the tips of them. It was dragging its wings. And it looked as if it had slept in its coat–a black coat that was too big.

Agatha turned around and walked along beside her grandmother. "It's ugly," she said again.

Her grandmother said, "It likes me. It follows me everywhere."

Agatha said, "Why is it still here? It's the middle of winter. All the other birds flew away long ago."

"Ravens are winter birds," her grandmother said. "They stay here all winter."

"It's stupid," Agatha said. "Stupid bird! Go away!" she yelled.

The bird screeched, "Crah!"

When Agatha went to bed that night, her grandmother said, "Put your boots under your pillow and your stockings inside your bed."

"Why?" Agatha asked.

Her grandmother said, "Because, if you leave your boots on the floor, they will be frozen solid by morning and you will not be able to put them on. If you keep your stockings inside your bed, they will stay warm and dry."

She thought about frozen boots and having very cold feet. "All right," she said.

She folded her sealskin kamiik and put them under her pillow and her stockings in her bed. It was a very cold winter, but her caribou-skin blankets were warm. She nestled deeper into her bed. She wondered where the ugly bird would sleep.

The next morning, there were two ravens. They were with the dogs, which were tied in a line. One raven—a huge, ugly bird – teased the dogs while the other stole some of the dogs' food. Then they flew. They flew up and down and around. They did loops and somersaults in the air, one raven flying right behind the other. They seemed to be having a good time.

"They're playing," Agatha thought. They were interesting, these ugly black birds.

They fought over the bit of food they had stolen. The big bird took the food and flew away with it. Her grandmother's bird did not get any food at all.

"Mean bird!" Agatha yelled at the big bird.

"Crah!" the big bird replied.

"Why is the small bird always here, Grandmother?" Agatha asked.

Her grandmother said, "Last winter, when it first came, it was small and it was sick. I fed it and it has stayed close to me ever since." Agatha's grandmother took some fish and said, "Take this outside and give it to him."

Agatha went outside and put the fish on the ground. "Here, Ugly Bird!" she yelled.

The bird hopped over, took the fish and hopped away with it. It began to eat but did not fly away. The other bird watched from a distance.

"Naa, naa, na, nanny; trying to be a meany; not getting any," Agatha teased the big black bird.

"Crah!" the bird replied.

From then on, when Agatha walked to her grandmother's hut, the bird would meet her along the way. "Hi, Ugly Bird," she would say. The bird would hop along behind her.

In spring, the sun stays in the sky day and night and the snow softens.

Up in the sky, the ravens played, flying around doing loops and somersaults. They had changed. The frost was gone from their beaks. They were so black they looked almost blue. Their feathers glistened in the sun. And their coats were no longer too big; they fit. They had become beautiful.

Agatha lay on her back, watching them. The ravens flew side by side. Then, the bird on the left turned itself upside down and flew under the other one—only for a moment, but she saw it. It fell away and righted itself. It caught up to its friend and did it again. She had never seen any bird do this before. These were the most amazing birds she had ever seen. She watched them for a long time.

One day, Agatha saw a little, round white bird with black wings: a qupanuaq, a snow bunting. Agatha always thought snow buntings were rather funny birds. They seem to jump into the air. They flap their wings really fast, they climb a bit and then they stop flapping and fall a bit. They flap again and stop. Up and down, up and down. She always laughed when she saw them.

The sandhill cranes came next, flying gracefully with their long wings. As they flew, they seemed to go flaa-ap, flaa-ap, giving that little extra flap at the end with their big wings. They walked on the hills, holding up their long necks, and cried, "Krr-krrr..." You could hear them from miles away.

There were seagulls. They were always hungry and they were noisy. They screamed, "Squawk, squawk!" Agatha decided she did not like gulls; they were too noisy. She liked quiet birds.

Sometimes as she walked, a golden plover would land beside her and run away, pretending to have a broken wing. They were silly. When Agatha ran after them, they always got better and flew away.

Other birds arrived: snow geese, Canada geese, ducks, loons and swans. Flocks of ptarmigans walked on the eskers.

The birds built nests. There were little birds everywhere. The little sigjariarjuits–sandpipers–were so cute. They looked like little tufts of grey fluff with long, skinny legs. They ran, staggering, fell over, got up and ran again. Sometimes there would be four or five of them, running everywhere.

Pairs of swans floated on the lakes with their little ones. Some of them bobbed up and down on the water with their beaks tucked under their wings. They were so peaceful. Agatha liked swans.

She looked for the ravens, but they were nowhere to be found. "Maybe they have flown away," she thought. She laughed. They were such funny birds, those ravens, spending the cold winter in Repulse Bay and flying away when spring and summer came.

But she did not miss the ravens. She thought about how they looked when they were ugly and she missed them even less. And now there were birds everywhere. Agatha watched the birds all summer long.

The grasses stood high, already turning brown, waving in the late summer breeze. The siksiit, ground squirrels, gathered food and took it into their holes in the ground. The young foxes turned white and young rabbits hopped about with their mothers, eating. Soon the polar bears would come and walk along the shore, waiting for the ice to form in the huge Hudson Bay.

The birds gathered in great numbers. Geese landed on the hillsides by the thousands. The sandhill cranes floated into the sky with their young, teaching them how to fly. The snow buntings flew around by the hundreds, pecking at the ground wherever they landed.

A thin layer of ice formed on the lakes every night and broke up every morning. The swans bobbed up and down among the waves.

Soon the geese were flying south, long Vs of them flying way, way up in the sky. Every day, all day long, Agatha watched the geese flying away by the thousands. The other birds too began to go away.

The little kajuqtaat, horned larks, brown birds with black cheeks, were the last to go. As the snow came, they ran around in the drifts, looking for food. They always stayed as long as they could. But before long they too were gone.

Winter had come. There were no birds left. Agatha was sad: all those beautiful birds had gone. She looked around. There was snow, there were dogs, there were igloos and huts, but nothing else. It was an empty, lonely place. Agatha wanted to sleep.

Then, one day as Agatha was walking to her grandmother's hut, she heard a most incredible sound: "Boi-yoi-yung!" It sounded like someone had hit a long piece of metal pipe with a rock. But there was no pipe anywhere.

"Boi-yoi-yung." Agatha heard the sound again.

She looked around. There, sitting on a rock, looking at the dogs and making this most incredible sound, was the ugliest bird she had ever seen. It was completely black except for the frost on the side of its beak. It looked as if it was wearing a coat that was two sizes too big.

Agatha smiled. She yelled, "Hi, Ugly Bird!"

"Crah!" the bird replied. "Boi-yoi-yoi-yung!"

The bird flew over and landed. It hopped along behind Agatha, dragging its wings on the ground. Agatha was happy. It would not be a lonely winter after all. The most amazing bird was back.

Taimakalauq

Agatha Goes to School

"Shh," Agatha said. "Listen."

We listened. Way in the distance we heard the sound of an airplane: "Drrrr..." We looked south to the horizon.

"Do you see it?" Agatha asked.

"No," Nick Amautinnuaq said. But we could hear it clearly now.

"There it is!" Andreasi said. "Just above the little island."

Agatha scrunched up her eyes and peered at the sky above the little island with the wooden pole sticking up on it. Sure enough, there it was, a small black dot, moving swiftly. Andreasi had very sharp eyes.

The airplane came closer and closer. "Drrrr..." It had wings on top and pontoons that looked like big, long silver fish hanging under it. It looked as if it was flying slightly sideways. Agatha thought airplanes always looked as if they were flying slightly sideways. "Drrrr..."

The airplane lifted its left wing and flew in a big circle. It came down, with a splash, on the sea. It floated among the waves, its propeller going round. The pilot came out, walked along the pontoon and tied a rope to a cleat at the back. The airplane gently beached itself in front of the Hudson's Bay Company store. The pilot jumped off and tied the other end of the rope to a big rock on the beach.

Agatha looked south and thought what a strange place it must be. There was a world she had only heard about, a place where people spoke English and the language-of-the-priests; a place where trees, what she called standing-ups, stood in the ground... For Agatha, it was a place of wonder. Today she would find out what it was like down there. Today she would get into this airplane and go south. She would go away to school in Chesterfield Inlet.

Agatha said goodbye to her parents. She would not see them again for a long time. She climbed into the airplane with Nick and Andreasi.

The pilot untied the airplane. He pushed it away from the beach and climbed inside. He sat down in his seat and started the engine. It was so loud that it shook. And it smelled of gas and oil. The plane took off and headed south. Agatha looked through the window. She could see the ground way down below. Everybody in the airplane sat feeling glum. Nick sat very still and looked straight ahead. Andreasi was crying. Agatha missed her mother and father. She had never been away from them before.

Chesterfield Inlet was a big place. Agatha had never seen so many houses before. There was a hospital, a school and a Catholic mission. Agatha had never seen such big buildings. But there were no standing-ups standing in the ground.

There were more people in this place than Agatha had seen in all her life. On the other side of the bay lived the Royal Canadian Mounted Police. They had their very own lake to get their water from. It was called the RCMP lake.

In summer, the RCMP collected their water from the lake in pails and carried it back to their houses. In the fall, they waited until the ice was fifteen centimetres thick and then they cut it into squares with big saws. They pulled the ice out with big tongs, and hauled it home on their sleds. They took the giant ice cubes into their houses, one by one, and melted them to use for water all winter long.

The priests did priestly things and the brothers were bakers and carpenters. The nuns, who were the most amazing of all, were mostly nurses, which is why, to this very day, nurses are called najannguat, pretending-to-be-nuns.

Agatha and her friends stayed in the attic of the Catholic mission with the nuns. The nuns did not make very good mothers and the priests, who were called fathers, did not make very good fathers. Agatha missed her mother and father. Sometimes, when she went to bed at night, Agatha cried herself to sleep.

Downstairs, there was a big church with a big rounded roof. At the back of the church, in the balcony, the nuns sang so beautifully that Agatha thought they must sound like angels.

But they were not angels. If you did not kneel just so and hold your hands just so in church, they would get mad and hit you on the knuckles. Agatha did not like to kneel just so; her knees hurt on the hard wooden pews. But her knuckles hurt more, so she knelt just so and held her hands just so and listened to the angels singing.

Agatha tried not to think bad thoughts; her mother would not want her to think bad thoughts. And besides, there were some good things that happened in this awful place where Agatha had to live, away from her mother and father.

For one thing, there were the skis. They appeared one day in the porch. Agatha liked them right away. She took a pair of them, went outside, strapped them to her moccasins and skied. It was fun. She skied along, fell in the snow, laughed, got up and skied on. After that day she would go to the hill near the RCMP lake and ski downhill. Agatha and her friends made bumps of snow on the hillside and bounced off them. Agatha laughed and laughed.

The boys walked from the mission with their mouths full of water. They climbed the hill, sat on the snow, spat the water on their hands and rubbed the water on the bottoms of their moccasins. They let the water freeze and slid down the hill on icy moccasins. They climbed up the hill on their hands and knees and slid down the hill again. It was fun. They all laughed and had a really good time.

And then there were the skates. They too appeared in the porch one day, a big pile of them. Agatha laced her skates on at the RCMP lake and tried to stand. She went a little way. And then her feet went right out from under her. She hit the ice with the back of her head, hard. Ice in October is really hard. Agatha saw stars rising up, straight into the sky; blue stars and red stars, yellow stars and green stars; stars of all colours coming from the back of her head, rising straight into the sky. Agatha's head hurt. Her feet hurt. She took her skates off. Agatha decided skating was dangerous. She would not skate anymore; she would ski.

Sometimes when you skate, the ice crackles. Lines form in all directions. That's when you know the ice is thin. But thin ice is fun to skate on, and the silly boys would skate on it. The nuns who took care of Agatha would say, "Stay away from thin ice! You might fall through."

Father Fafard was not a silly boy. He was a plump priest with a round face, a white beard and moustache and a long black robe. He smelled like a cigar. He too would say, "Stay away from thin ice. You might fall in."

One evening after school, Agatha and her friends went to the RCMP lake. Nick brought his skates. Andreasi brought his skates. But Agatha skied. Nick said, "Why are you skiing? We're going skating."

Agatha said, "I don't want to skate. Skates hurt my feet. I fall and my head hurts. I want to ski."

Nick said, "Sissy!"

Father Fafard was the greatest skater in the world. And he knew it. He skated toward Agatha very fast – too fast. Agatha thought he was going to hit her. But Father Fafard did not hit Agatha; he turned in the nick of time and glided ever so gracefully in another direction, his arms stretched out like a ballet dancer.

Agatha laughed. Father Fafard laughed. He was showing off. He would skate at the boys and girls and turn in the nick of time. Everybody had a good time.

Father Fafard jumped and turned in mid-air. He spun like a top, his black robes puffed up all around him, his black cross, with Jesus nailed to it, swinging around him. He did a graceful pirouette. Then he went across the ice, backwards, cutting a perfect arc with his sharp skates. There was a loud "Crack, crack, craaackk!!" And Father Fafard went through the ice.

The RCMP had been cutting ice blocks for their water that morning. There was a big spot of thin ice in the middle of the lake. It was cold and the lake had frozen over. But Agatha and her friends were not very heavy, whereas Father Fafard was plump and heavy, and the ice could not hold him. He fell through the ice. And there he was, his puffed-up black robes floating in the water like black bubbles all around him.

"Ugh, ugh, ugh..." he said, his teeth beginning to chatter.

He looked up and there was Nick Amautinnuaq standing there with a big smile on his face. Someone giggled. Father Fafard said, "It's, it's, it's c-c-co-olld!"

He smiled a slightly embarrassed smile. Agatha smiled tentatively. She started to laugh. Then everyone laughed and laughed.

Father Fafard tried to climb out of the water. The ice was slippery with water and more of it broke. He tried again. And again the ice broke. No matter how hard he tried, Father Fafard could not get out of the water. Nick reached out to Father Fafard, but he was too far away and was afraid of falling into the water.

"I can't reach him," Nick said. "What shall we do?"

"What shall we do?" Andreasi said.

Agatha came over on her skis. "I can reach him," she said.

"You? How can you reach him?" Nick said. "You're just a little girl."

"With my skis," Agatha said. "I can reach him with my skis."

Agatha took off her skis. "Hold onto my feet," she said to Nick.

Agatha got down on her stomach, holding her skis in her hands. She reached out to Father Fafard with her skis. "Grab these, Father Fafard," she said.

Father Fafard grabbed the other end of the skis.

"Pull yourself up," Agatha said.

Slowly Father Fafard inched his way up the skis until he was on top of the ice.

"Pull!" Agatha said.

Nick pulled on Agatha's feet. Andreasi pulled on Nick's feet. All three of them pulled along until Father Fafard was on the thick ice. Father Fafard shivered.

"We'd better get him inside," Agatha said.

They walked with Father Fafard to the mission house and left him with the priests to warm up. Poor man; his watch and his glasses were lost, resting on the muddy bottom of the RCMP lake. But he was happy, even though he could not see very well.

And he never showed off again. Well, maybe a little. He really was a very good skater.

Taima

Afterword

Agatha is a made-up girl. I have a friend named Agatha who lives in Repulse Bay, but she is not the girl in these stories; I just like her name. So I used it. But everything else, well, almost everything else, that happens in these stories is true.

My old grandmother died about 10 years ago. I don't know how old she was but she was so old that she refused to live a modern life. She lived in her tent just outside her house all summer long, and her own room, inside her house, was made up just like her tent, with water bucket, Coleman stove and teapot. One day I saw her walking with a raven hopping along behind her. I asked her about it and she said, "I fed it one day and it has been following me around ever since." I thought it was a neat idea for a story.

In 1954, when I was six years old, an airplane came and took me away to school in Chesterfield Inlet. Some of my friends came too, Agatha, Nick and Andreasi among them. It was not a happy time. I missed my mother, my father and my brothers and sisters, and I cried the whole year. But my mother has always told me not to think bad thoughts.

Many people who went to that school have now charged the Catholic Church, the Government of Canada and all those involved with harassing boys and girls. Some of the priests, brothers and nuns who took care of us are now gone. And I am sure some of them have not gone to heaven. But there were some good things that happened; we got a good education. And then there were the skis, the skates and Father Fafard. If he is not with us any longer, I am sure he has gone to heaven.

Taima

Some words you've seen in this book:

amautinnuaq (AHM-ah-oo-TEEN-oo-ahk) — woman's coat for carrying babies

avataq (AHV-ah-tahk) — an inflated sealskin used in hunting whales and seals

kajuqtaat (kah-YOOK-tah-aht) — horned larks

kamiik (KAH-mee-eek) — waterproof sealskin boots

najannguat (nah-YANNG-goo-aht) —pretending-to-be-nuns (nurses)

qaaqtaqtut (ka-AHK-tahk-toot)—exploding-things

qupanuaq (koo-PAH-noo-ahk) — snow bunting

sigjariarjuit (SEEGH-yar-ee-AR-yoo-eet) — sandpipers

siksiit (SEEK-see-eet)—ground squirrels

taima (tah-EE-ma) — that's all

taimakalauq (tah-EE-ma-KAH-la-ook) — that's all for now

tulugarjuaq (too-loo-GAR-yoo-ahk) — raven

uugait (OO-gah-eet)—tiny bearded fish